Nathan
&
Nicholas Alexander

by Lulu Delacre

SCHOLASTIC INC.
New York   Toronto   London   Auckland   Sydney

To Verónica, with love

a Lucas • Evans Book

ISBN 0-590-41573-5

20 19 18 17 16   6/9

Printed in the U.S.A.   23

$\mathcal{O}$ne night . . .

while Nathan was fast asleep,

some very strange noises
came out of his toy chest.
Swish, swish, swish . . .
brrrm, clack, pop, click,
BANG!

So he turned on the light and took a big breath.
Then he crept toward the toy chest . . .

and peeked inside.

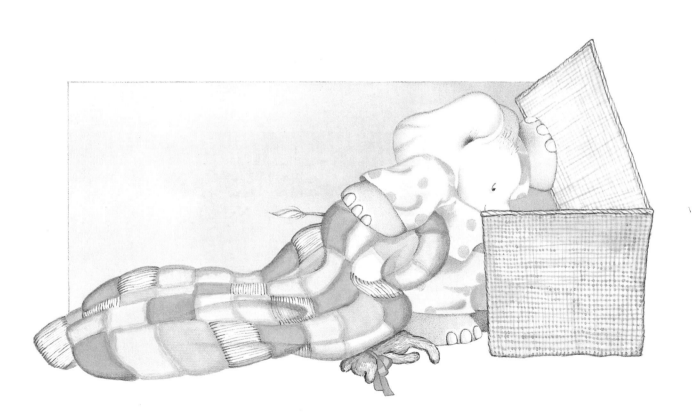

"Ooouuch!" Nathan cried,
after receiving a painful bite
on his snout.

"Excuse me, sir,
but you quite frightened me.
Besides, don't you know
it is in very bad taste
to enter someone's home
without knocking first?"

"But that is my toy chest!"
Nathan replied.
"I've just moved in
so if you don't mind,
now it's my house as well.
And by the way,
let me introduce myself properly.
My name, sir, is
Nicholas Alexander."

"I come from a family
that lived among kings,
dwelled in high castles,
and told tales to the queen.
Of fairies and dragons,
I know quite a lot, sir!"

"I don't care, Mr. Alexander,
where you came from," said Nathan.
"This is *my* toy chest."

"Oh, please call me Nicholas.
And now . . ."

"I really must do my cleaning before the night is over."

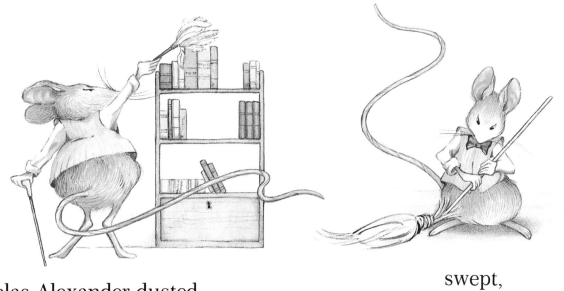

Nicholas Alexander dusted,

swept,

and polished.

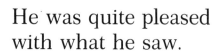

He was quite pleased
with what he saw.

Nathan was not.

"This toy chest is *mine*!" he cried.
"Couldn't you share it with a friend?"
"No!" shouted Nathan.

He grabbed Nicholas Alexander
and flung him across the room.

Then Nathan looked inside the toy chest.
It was divided into two equal parts.
Over each hung a tiny sign
with beautiful gold letters.
One sign said NICHOLAS ALEXANDER.
The other said NATHAN.

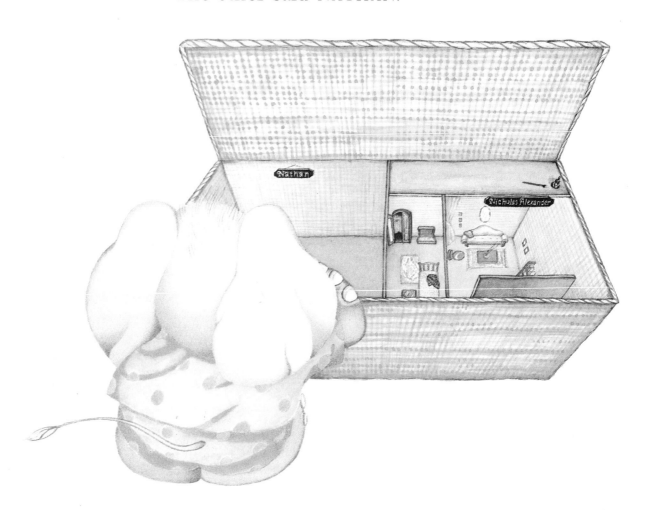

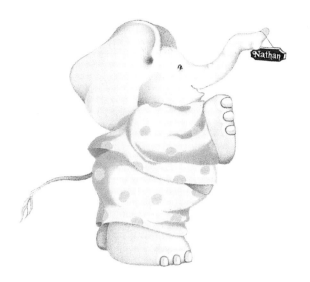

Nathan read his name
letter by letter.

"I like it!"
he said.

Mr. Alexander really does
know quite a lot, he thought.

"Maybe it would be nice
to have him as a friend."

"He could show me how to write my name
in teeny tiny letters!
Really fancy ones with golden ink.
He could help me with my homework.
And I could show him how to do puzzles. . . .
We could even read my books together!"

"Mr. Alexander! I mean Nicholas. . . ."

"I'm sorry I got angry," said Nathan.
"That's quite all right, sir,
it happens to the best of friends."
"Then you would still like to be my friend?" asked Nathan.
"Of course," said Nicholas. "I think we shall get on quite well."

"Now about the fishing trip
I've planned for tomorrow morning. . . ."
"A fishing trip!" cried Nathan.
"I've never been on a fishing trip before."
"Just one of the many things
we will be doing," said Nicholas.

"It's late now and your toys
need putting away."

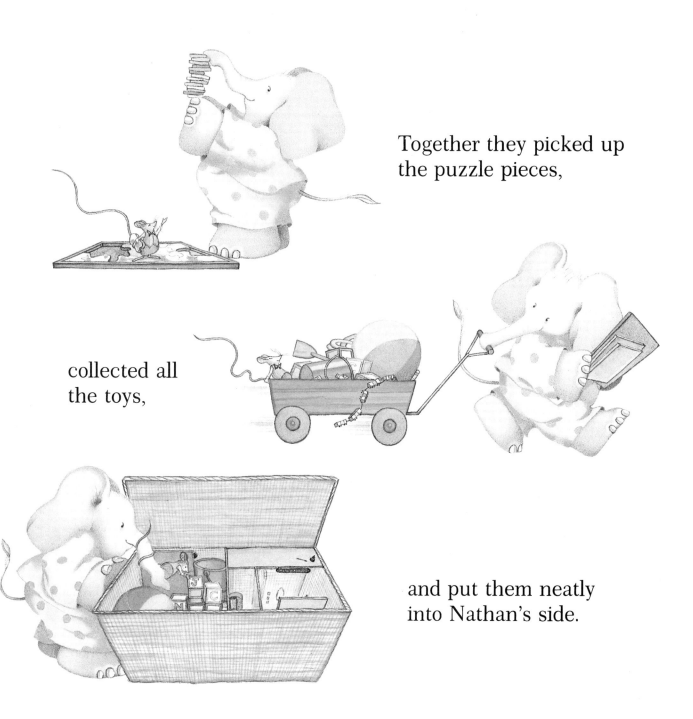

Together they picked up
the puzzle pieces,

collected all
the toys,

and put them neatly
into Nathan's side.

It was well into the night.
A full moon shone in the sky.
They were both rather sleepy.
It had been quite an evening.

As Nathan snuggled into bed,
he whispered across the room,
"Nicholas!
This is not the end
of a dream, is it?"
"No," said a muffled little voice.
"No, sir. This is the beginning
of an extraordinary friendship."

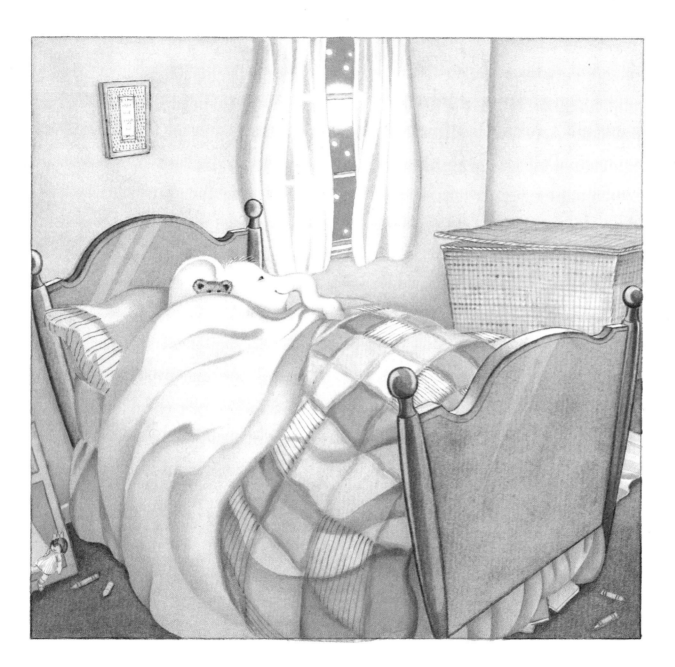